CL295831

While these two poems are quite separate, they have many similar features and lead on naturally from each other. Some scholars even think they may be linked. To make this version, for children now, I have joined the two together (at Chapter 5), left out one episode from the first poem, added some opening paragraphs and lengthened the very abrupt ending.

Throughout, I have tried to stay as true to the spirit of the original as possible and, wherever I could, to keep close to the original text, which, since I don't read Sumerian or cuneiform, means the academic, line-by-line translations. Enormous distances of time and understanding stretch between us and this story. The Sumerian poetry is rich, dense and full of mysteries. How old was Lugalbanda? Was Enmerkar his father? What about the riddle of the goddess at the end? What happened?

In trying to tell this story for today I have, of course, made choices and interpretations, simplified some things, emphasized or omitted others. For all this, the responsibility is mine alone. None of it would have been possible without the incredible work of the scholars and experts who have brought these extraordinary poems back into our world. My debt to them is immeasurable. And my hope is that this version will do their work justice and bring the story of Lugalbanda to life again for young people of the twenty-first century.

K. H.

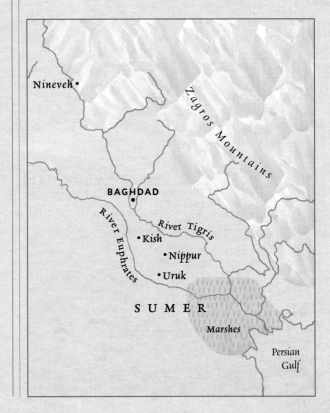

LUGALBANDA

THE·BOY·WHO·GOT
CAUGHT·UP·IN·A·WAR

LUGALBANDA

THE·BOY·WHO·GOT
CAUGHT·UP·IN·A·WAR

KATHY HENDERSON

illustrated by

JANE RAY

WALKER BOOKS
AND SUBSIDIARIES
LONDON · BOSTON · SYDNEY · AUCKLAND

First published 2006 by Walker Books Ltd
87 Vauxhall Walk, London SE11 5HJ

10 9 8 7 6 5 4 3 2 1

Text © 2006 Kathy Henderson   Illustrations © 2006 Jane Ray

The right of Kathy Henderson and Jane Ray to be identified as author
and illustrator respectively of this work has been asserted by them in
accordance with the Copyright, Designs and Patents Act 1988

This book has been typeset in Rialto DF

Printed in China

British Library Cataloguing in Publication Data:
a catalogue record for this book is
available from the British Library

ISBN-13: 1-978-1-84428-746-8
ISBN-10: 1-84428-746-7

www.walkerbooks.co.uk

For the children of the Tigris and Euphrates.

In memory of Jeremy Black.

K.H. & J.R.

We would like to thank Fran Hazelton, an

English-speaking Mesopotamian story-teller,

for introducing us to this story and for her advice

and encouragement; Stephanie Dalley and the late

Jeremy Black of Oxford University and

Dominique Collon of The British Museum

for their help and support; and the

Electronic Text Corpus of Sumerian Literature

and all who work on it for invaluable source

material at www-etcsl.orient.ox.ac.uk.

THIS·IS·THE·STORY· of a boy called Lugalbanda who got caught up in a war. It is one of the oldest stories in the world, older than the Torah, the Bible, the Koran, older than Homer or the Greek and Roman myths, older even than the Epic of Gilgamesh. Told aloud five thousand years ago and more, it comes from the land of Ancient Sumer, which we now call Iraq.

Sumer lay on the hot, flat plains between two great rivers, the Tigris and the Euphrates. This was good land. Baked by the sun and watered by the slow-flowing rivers, the crops grew thick and fast.

The Sumerians were skilful. They dug canals and streams to carry the river water in all directions so they could grow fields of barley. They planted vines and vegetables, herbs and spices, apple, fig and pomegranate trees under the tall date palms. They raised flocks of sheep, cows and goats for food and caught fish and wildfowl in the rivers. For the first time people had more food than they needed, lots more, enough for many to live in the same place and still have some left over.

Taking clay from the ground, the Sumerians made pots for storing their surplus oil and grain. They made clay bricks and paving-slabs and more. And with these they made buildings, great temples to the gods who ruled their world, and storerooms for their precious food supplies. They built paved streets and houses and palaces for their kings, who did the gods' work on earth, and round them they built huge protecting walls. The Sumerians created cities. And on the banks of the Euphrates, Uruk, the city in this story, was one of the first and greatest of them all.

There was another first to which we owe this story. Taking lumps of clay, the Sumerians pressed them out flat and made rows of wedge-shaped marks in the soft surface with sharpened reeds, making marks that looked like birds' footprints. This was the world's first writing, called cuneiform.

And that is how, some time around four and a half thousand years ago, this story, which had already been passed from story-teller to story-teller for longer than anyone could remember, came to be written down as two poems on clay tablets and baked hard in the hot sun. And for many years after, scribes passing on the strange new craft of writing copied it down again and again.

But four and a half thousand years is a very long time. The cities with their stores and treasure-troves were raided, ruined, rebuilt, conquered again. New people came and the Sumerians slowly disappeared, their language replaced by other languages, their libraries of clay tablets buried under mounds of rubble, meaningless. In time, even cuneiform writing died out.

For four thousand years this story was lost.

Then, a mere hundred and fifty years or so ago, curious travellers, seeing the strange mounds sticking out of the flat land, began to dig. They found the remains of walls and temples and cities. They found heaps of broken clay slabs with strange marks on them. What did they mean?

Patiently and brilliantly, many scholars in different countries worked away at the puzzle of the tablets and bit by bit they worked out first the writing, then the language until, at last, and only very recently, this story was pieced together again.

So here, for the first time ever in our days of paper and print, is the story of Lugalbanda told for a new generation. Lugalbanda, whose name, translated literally, means "little prince"; Lugalbanda, who grew up to be one of the great kings of Uruk and Sumer and the father of the hero Gilgamesh; Lugalbanda, the boy who got caught up in a war.

Here is one of the oldest stories in the world, brand new.

A very long time ago, in the land now called Iraq, there lived a little prince whose name was Lugalbanda. His home was the great city of Uruk, famous for its brick buildings, its paved streets and for the black-haired men and women who lived there. Their ruler was powerful King Enmerkar.

In those days there were many gods in the world and everything that happened, happened because of them. There was a sun-god, a moon-god, a god of earth, a sky-god, a god of dreams, a god of animals, and many, many more. But one of the greatest of them all was Inana, the goddess of love and war; Inana, the evening star. She chose the kings. It was she who had called on Enmerkar when he was a young man to drain the land and build a city where once there were only marshes and reeds. Inana was his guardian, and Uruk her home among men.

King Enmerkar was proud of his city. He wanted it to be the best in all the world and he was always looking for ways to make it greater. But he was troubled because far away, beyond the wild mountains that rose up from the plains like the wall of the land, he knew there was another city, the legendary city of Aratta.

Aratta had stone and stone-masons who carved it. Aratta had artists in silver and gold. Aratta had metals, precious stones and blue lapis lazuli. And Uruk did not.

"I must conquer that proud place," said the king, as powerful rulers will, "reduce it to rubble and bring all its treasures and its works of art back here so that Uruk, and Uruk alone, will be the greatest city in the world. Glory be to Inana!"

And he began to prepare for war.

Lugalbanda was young and weak, but he had seven older brothers. They were fine young men in the prime of life and each of

these seven princes was a commander in the king's army. Lugalbanda loved and admired his brothers more than anything in the world. Everything that they did he wanted to do too.

So when King Enmerkar's heralds blew their horns to summon every man in the land to join the war against Aratta, Lugalbanda was determined to go with them.

For days men flocked to the city in answer to the king's call. They covered the ground like heavy fog and stirred up a cloud of dust so big it whirled up into the sky. Their shields clattered. Their spears spiked the air. And when at last the great army was ready, they marched out through the city gates behind King Enmerkar with his armour gleaming and the standard of Uruk held high. They stormed through the fields of barley that surrounded the city and away across the plains like a herd of wild bulls.

And Lugalbanda went with them. ❖

·T·W·O·

They marched for a day. They marched for two days. Further from the city with every step, they marched for three, four and five days more. At night they made camp and lit fires on the ground and baked bread on the hot stones.

On the sixth day they came to a river where they bathed and rested. In front of them loomed a terrible range of mountains. The soldiers looked up at the rocky peaks and spoke in frightened whispers. These were unknown places, dangerous wastes where monsters lurked and no one could survive alone. On the seventh day they marched into the mountains in hushed silence.

Up they marched for days and days and days, deep into the Zabu Mountains where the cypress trees grow, and there, suddenly, the little prince fell ill. His head twitched like a strangled snake. His hands lost their grip.

He couldn't take another step, but fell to the ground like a snared gazelle, and his mouth bit the dirt.

For all his mighty army, there was nothing King Enmerkar could do. His troops, massed

on the mountainside like a great dust-cloud, were just as helpless. Lugalbanda's brothers were desperate.

"We must take him back to Uruk!" said one.

"How can we?" said another.

"We have to get him back to the palace!"

"But how?"

Lugalbanda's teeth were chattering in the

mountain cold. His brothers carried him to a warm cave and tried to make him comfortable.

They made a soft place for him to lie, like a great bird's nest, and laid out chunks of plump meat, sheep's cheese, bread, butter

and hard-boiled eggs. They brought jars of syrup, baskets of dates and sweetmeats to tempt him to eat. They filled leather bags with provisions and water-skins with beer and wine. They hung pots of scented incense over Lugalbanda's head, and beside him they laid his axe made of tin and his dagger made of iron.

Outside the king and his army were getting impatient.

The little prince lay there senseless. His lips were dry. His face was burning. His eyes stared blankly and tears ran down his cheeks like water bubbling from a spring. His brothers lifted his head but he didn't seem to be breathing.

"What can we do?" they asked each other. "We can't stay here. We have to go on. War won't wait."

"If we leave him," said one, "maybe he'll recover. Maybe he'll rise from his bed like the sun rises in the morning. And if Lugalbanda eats and drinks the things we've left for him, his strength will come back and then, maybe, the sun-god Utu will lead him back over the

mountains, back to the city of Uruk and home." But he sighed.

"Yes," said another, "but what if he doesn't recover? What if the sun-god Utu summons him to the next life and his strength leaves him for ever?"

"Then it will be up to us to fetch his body when we come back from Aratta and carry it home over the mountains to the city of Uruk ourselves."

Outside the trumpets sounded. The army was starting to move.

Bowed down with grief, the seven princes left their little brother behind, there in the cave in the Zabu Mountains where the cypress trees grow, and marched away weeping with the army of King Enmerkar, on to conquer Aratta.

·T·H·R·E·E·

Lugalbanda lay in the mountain cave for two whole days and nights. All through the third day he lay there, until, just as the sun was setting and the evening air was growing sharp and cold, he woke up sweating as if he'd been covered in oil.

"Oh Sun-god Utu," he sobbed as he saw the sun going down, "you led me into these mountains with my brothers. Please don't leave me all alone in this cave. I have no one to comfort me: no mother, no father, no brothers, no friends. Please don't let me die alone in the Zabu Mountains where the cypress trees grow. Sun-god Utu, don't let me die!"

The sun-god heard his pleas and, beaming his last rays of the evening into the cave, he let him live. Then he was gone.

The evening star appeared, the great goddess Inana, guardian of the city of Uruk.

"Great Inana," Lugalbanda cried, "I want to go home! Take me back to the city, back to my mother and to Uruk with its brick-built palaces and paved streets and the sound of voices and laughter. Don't leave me here all alone in this cave. Please take me home!"

The goddess heard him. She shone her light into the cave and, wrapping the little prince's heart in joy like a soft wool blanket, she sent him off to sleep.

Then she went back to Uruk.

The moon rose slowly in the sky. Bathing the cave in silver light, Nanna-Suen the moon-god came to watch over Lugalbanda.

The little prince woke and whispered to the moon, "Oh Nanna-Suen, stay with me now and give me back my strength." And the moon-god heard his prayer and gave his legs the power to stand.

When at last the young sun-god Utu appeared on the horizon with a new day, Lugalbanda got unsteadily to his feet and walked out into the morning.

Life-giving plants sprang up around him in the warmth of the sun, and mountain streams brought healing water to his side. The little prince sighed with relief. "Oh Sun-god Utu, when you sleep, we sleep too. When you rise, we come back to life. You make everything happen. How sweet it is to praise you!" And Lugalbanda ate the plants and drank the water and began to mend. ❖

·F·O·U·R·

That evening, as his strength returned, Lugalbanda set off to find his brothers. Like a wild horse, he picked his way up the steep rocks, looking here, looking there, looking everywhere for the army of King Enmerkar.

But there was no sign of it. When night fell, the empty mountains were like a wasteland in the moonlight and, even to his bright eyes, there was no one to be seen.

Lugalbanda thought about his brothers. They had had fires and freshly baked bread at the end of the day's march. I should do the same, he thought. But how? He had carried the leather bags of provisions with him from the cave; now he stopped and looked inside. He took out a pair of flint-stones and gathered up grass and sticks into a pile. How was it done? He banged the two stones together. Nothing happened. He tried again. Still nothing. Again and again he tried and finally a spark leapt, a wisp of smoke, a tiny glow. Soon Lugalbanda had made a fire that shone out through the dark like the sun.

Now what? thought the little prince. I don't know how to bake and I don't have an oven, but maybe... Searching the leather bags again, he mixed some things he found there with water and kneaded them into a dough. Then he divided it into round pieces and put them to bake beside the fire while he went to find broad leaves from the mountain reeds to wrap them in.

The air soon filled with delicious smells. Were they cooked? Lugalbanda poured honey-herb and date syrup over the hot cakes and then he took a bite. Oh, what a taste! These were the best cakes he'd ever eaten. Heavenly sweet!

Next day the little prince set off again with his cakes wrapped in leaves in the bag on his back. On he went, higher and higher, aching with loneliness, but there was still no trace of his brothers. Soon he had left the trees behind and even barer, bleaker, steeper slopes stretched away in front of him. These were the Lullubu Mountains where no cypress trees grow, where no snakes slither and no scorpions scurry.

When Lugalbanda lay down to sleep in the dark of that night, there was not a sign of life. He was all alone and quite, quite lost. ❖

In the Lullubu Mountains where no cypress trees grow, where no snakes slither and no scorpions scurry, where the little prince slept and the night was dark, the multi-coloured mountain of the goddess Inana rises like a tower higher than all the others. At its top grows a tree so big its branches cloak the mountain slopes in shade and its roots drink like snakes from the seven mouths of the rivers far below. And near this tree on the rocks on the ground was the nest of the terrible Anzu bird.

The Anzu bird was a monster of the skies. It had the teeth of a shark and the talons of an eagle. When it took to the air, its wings blocked out the sun. Wild bulls fled into the foothills for fear of it. Wild stags scattered to the high peaks to try and escape its clutches.

Now, as the night came to an end and a new day began, high in its nest the Anzu bird stretched out its wings and let out a cry that rocked the ground.

Lugalbanda woke with a jolt. He opened his eyes and what did he see but the terrible Anzu bird beating its wings in its nest high above. And then... Did he quake? Did he quail? Did he run? Did he hide? No.

Lugalbanda the Brave sat and stared, and into his head came a brilliant idea.

What a bird! What a size! How high he must fly! thought the little prince. He must be able to see for miles. A creature like this must be treated with respect. I shall honour him. I'll give his family a treat, and if I please him and make him happy, surely he will show me the way to the king's army and my brothers!

So Lugalbanda stayed out of sight and waited until at last the Anzu bird and his wife flew off to go hunting, leaving their one and only chick all alone in the nest. Then, very quietly, he crept up the mountain, over the rocks, past the great tree, all the way up to the Anzu bird's nest, and there among the branches of juniper and box sat the Anzu chick.

The chick looked at Lugalbanda. Lugalbanda looked at the chick. He opened his leather bag and took out meats and treats and his own-made, honey-sweet cakes and laid them out in front of it. The chick opened its beak wide. Lugalbanda fed it salt meat and titbits of sheep fat. He tucked it into its nest. And then he made the chick beautiful by painting its eyes with black kohl eye-liner and putting a garland of scented white cedar on its head. He hung a twist of salt-beef on a branch, and every time the chick opened its gaping beak, he dropped another of his heavenly sweet cakes inside.

Then the little prince crept softly away and hid behind the rocks to wait. ❖

The Anzu bird was hunting hard,
hounding wild bulls across
the mountains,
snatching them
up from the
ground as they ran.
Before long the skies
darkened and
he flew into sight,
blocking out the sun,
with a live bull struggling in
his talons and a dead bull slung across
his shoulders, spitting bile by the beakful.
As he drew nearer, he called to his chick
as he always did.

"Raaaark!
Craaaark!"

he called. But the chick didn't reply.
Its beak was too full of cake.

The Anzu
bird was alarmed.
His chick always replied!
"Raaaark!
Craaaaaark!"
he called again.
Still no answer. "What's wrong?
What's happened to my chick?"
shrieked the Anzu bird.
"AIEEEEEE!"
his cry of grief reached
up to the heavens.
"Fear hangs over my nest
like the cattle pens before the slaughter!"

"AIEEEEEE!" shrieked his wife, and her cry of pain reached down to the earth and drove the gods of the mountains to hide like ants in the cracks of the ground.

The Anzu bird flew closer and closer until at last he could see his nest. But what was this? It looked like the home of a god! There were the cakes and the treats and the sweetmeats. There were the decorations. There was the twist of salt-beef hanging from a branch. And there, tucked up in the middle, sat his one and only, precious Anzu chick, fat and full of honey cakes, its eyes painted with kohl and sprigs of scented white cedar on its head.

"Who has done this wonderful thing?" crowed the Anzu bird. "I guard the Lullubu Mountains. I bar the way to the mountains like a great door. I decide the destiny of rolling rivers. Make yourself known, whoever you are! If you are a god, I shall be your friend. If you are a man, I shall fix your fate. For I am the guardian of the Lullubu Mountains and you shall have no enemies here!"

Trembling with fright and delight, Lugalbanda crept out of his hiding place and he sang the praises of the Anzu bird.

"Oh Anzu bird with the sparkling eyes,
  You wheel in the sky like a bather in a pool,
  You have heaven at your head and earth at your feet,
  Your wings are as wide as the winds can reach,
  And your spine is straight and your claws are strong,
  And your feathers like a garden to look upon."

He bowed to the ground. "Oh Anzu," he said, "my name is Lugalbanda and I have been waiting for you since yesterday. I am lost, here in the Lullubu Mountains where no cypress trees grow, searching for my brothers and the army of King Enmerkar, and I beg for your protection. Please be my father, your wife my mother, and your chick my brother. I lay my life before you: you shall decide my fate."

The Anzu bird was delighted with all this. "Lugalbanda, my Lugalbanda," he said, puffing himself up, "I shall reward you! You shall go back to your city like a conquering hero with your head held high. You shall sail in a flotilla like a ship full of silver, like a boat heavy with a harvest of apples, like a barge heaped full of golden grain, like a boat piled so high with cucumbers it casts a shadow in the sun!"

And Lugalbanda? He shook his head.

"No thank you." That was what he said.

"Well," said the Anzu bird. "Then you shall have arrows barbed like sunbeams, arrows sharp as moonbeams, magic arrows that bite like vipers, darts that bring death to everyone they strike. You shall bundle them up like piles of logs."

Again the little prince shook his head. "No thank you," Lugalbanda said.

"Take the armour of the gods then," said the Anzu bird, "the Lion-of-Battle helmet to protect your head, the breastplate of No-Retreat-in-the-Mountains and the battle-net that never fails. Take these!"

Still Lugalbanda shook his head.

"No. No. No thank you," was all he said.

"The god Dumuzi's butter churn?" said the Anzu bird. "Then you'll have the fat of the land and the cream of everything."

"No thank you," Lugalbanda said, "no," and "no," again. And his "no-no-no-no" echoed round the rocks like the call of a wild bird.

"Now you be careful, my Lugalbanda," the Anzu bird snapped at last. "Even a stubborn ox can be made to plough! Even a donkey can be made to go! I said I would grant you your wish no matter what, but everything I offer you refuse. So tell me, what is it that you want?"

And what do you think the little prince replied, this boy who'd been so weak and ill?

"Mighty Anzu bird," he said, "all I want is to be able to run: to have strength in my legs so I never get tired, and arms that can reach out and never feel weak. I want to dance like the sunlight, leap like a flame and dart like lightning, so I can go wherever I want to go and find my heart's desire. And if anyone curses me when I get back to my city, I hope that they get no joy of it and that no one will pick a fight with me because they think

I'm weak." He looked up at the monstrous bird towering over him, "And then I shall have woodcarvers make breathtaking statues of you, and you shall be famous all over the land to the glory of the gods of the temples!"

"Well!" said the Anzu bird. "Well! Well! Well!" And he fluffed up his feathers. "You shall have your wish. You shall have strength in your legs so you can run for ever and never get tired. You shall stretch out your arms and never feel weak. You shall dance like the sunlight, leap like a flame and dart like lightning so you can go wherever you want to go to find your heart's desire. And if anyone curses you when you get back to your city, they'll get no joy from it and no one will pick a fight with you because they think you're weak." The Anzu bird preened himself. "And then woodcarvers will make breathtaking

statues of me, the Anzu bird, and I will be famous throughout the land to the glory of the gods of the temples!" And the great bird shook out his wings. "Now to find your brothers and the army of King Enmerkar."

The Anzu bird flew up, up, up into the sky. Lugalbanda walked down, down, down the steep slopes. From high above, the Anzu bird saw King Enmerkar's army in the distance. From down below, Lugalbanda saw the dust-cloud they raised spiralling up into the air.

"Just a word of warning," the Anzu bird called, wheeling round again. "Don't tell your brothers or your friends or anyone at all about the fate I have fixed for you: fair fortune can conceal foul." He turned back towards the high peaks. "Now I must go to my nest, and you to your army." And the Anzu bird was gone. ❖

That was how Lugalbanda, like a pelican emerging from the reeds, returned to the world from the high places and walked into the middle of his brothers' troops.

"Lugalbanda!" his brothers cried, amazed.

"Lugalbanda!" And they hugged and kissed him. "You've come back! You've come back from the land of no return, from the mountains where no one dares to go alone! We'd given you up for lost!"

The seven princes gathered round their little brother like a flock of chattering birds. "But how did you cross the wide mountain rivers?" "Did you drink them up?" "How did you survive?"

"I stepped over the rivers," said Lugalbanda, choosing his words carefully. "I drank from their waters. I snarled like a wolf. I pecked at the ground like a wild pigeon and ate mountain acorns." But he didn't say a word about the Anzu bird or the fate he had made for him.

His brothers fussed over the boy as if he were a chick in the nest, feeding him and giving him things to drink. They hugged him and kissed him some more and drove the last sickness away from Lugalbanda the Pure. ❖

The next day King Enmerkar's army, with the seven princes in the lead, continued on its way, winding through the valleys like a snake in a grain pile. And Lugalbanda went with them.

Now at last they came in sight of the city of Aratta, famous for its stone and its metals, for its craftsmen and its beautiful things, and there they pitched their camp at the city boundary, expecting to conquer it in a matter of days.

But their tents were barely up when spears began to rain down on them from above and more stones than a year of raindrops pelted from the slingshots on the city walls.

The bombardment went on for hours. Hours became days. Before they knew it, days became weeks, weeks became months, and the year turned full circle. The crops grew tall and ripened around them until a yellow harvest stood beneath the sky.

Uruk's soldiers stared uneasily. Why weren't they winning? What had gone wrong? In front of them, the city of Aratta barred the way. They couldn't go forward. Behind them, like a wall of thorns, stood the terrible mountains where no one can survive alone. They couldn't go back.

King Enmerkar was troubled too, upset, afraid even. He called on Inana the goddess of love and war, Inana his guardian and guide. Again and again the old king called, but she wouldn't come to him.

So he went to his foot soldiers. "Who will carry a message across the mountains to Uruk for me, to the goddess Inana?" But no one came forward.

He went to his special troops. "Who will carry a message across the mountains to Uruk for me, to the goddess Inana?" But no one came forward.

He went to the commanders of his army, to Lugalbanda's seven brothers. "Who will carry a message across the mountains to Uruk for me, to the goddess Inana?" But still no one came forward.

King Enmerkar stood before the city of Aratta, wringing his hands, when out of the crowd stepped a boy. It was Lugalbanda.

"I'll carry the message for you," he said, bowing to the ground.

The king looked down at the little prince. "You?" he said, raising an eyebrow.

"Yes," said Lugalbanda. "But I must go alone."

The king raised both eyebrows. "The mountains are full of terrors. No one goes there alone."

Lugalbanda was silent. He bowed again and turned to leave.

"Wait," said the king. ❖

King Enmerkar called the whole army together in a great assembly and there, in front of all his men, he handed the precious standard of Uruk to Lugalbanda.

"Here, take the emblems of our city," he said, "and don't let them out of your hands. The honour and the courage of our kingdom rest with you. When you reach Uruk, take this message to my beloved goddess Inana. Once, long ago, she summoned me to Uruk when it was just a marsh. She had me drain the land and build the city and rule the people with justice and peace. All this I did as she asked. For fifty years I built. For fifty years I gave judgements. And now she has abandoned me, here of all places. Why? Why has she left me and gone back to Uruk? What have I done?"

The king went on, "Beg the great goddess Inana, beg her on your knees that even if she has no further use for me she will at least bring us all safely home to Uruk. Then I will lay down my spear and she can break my shield and I will make an end to war."

Lugalbanda took the standard of Uruk in his hand and the message in his mind and went to gather up a few provisions for his journey.

As he approached, his brothers snapped at him as if he were a stray dog trying to join their pack. "Who do you think you are?" they said. "Carrying the royal standard! You're much too young. Let someone else go to Uruk!"

But the little prince was proud. "I shall go for Enmerkar, son of Utu. And I shall go alone." How he spoke to them!

"At least take someone with you," said his brothers, their hearts sinking. "The journey's full of dangers. If the gods don't watch over you, we'll never see you again, never hold you in our arms, never stand on the same ground or live in the same house again. You'll never come back from the terrible mountains where no one goes alone."

But Lugalbanda stood firm. "I've given my word," he said, "and time is passing. No one can go with me across the wide earth."

And with that he left.

·T·E·N·

As soon as he was out of sight, the little prince began to run. From the foot of the valley he ran, up into the high mountains. He ran over one mountain, over two, three, four, five, six and seven mountains. He ran like the wind and his legs were strong and he never got tired, and before it was even midnight once, he came to Uruk and the temple where the goddess Inana sat on her cushion.

Lugalbanda threw himself on the ground before the goddess. She greeted him with joy, as tenderly as if he were her husband or her son. "How did you come here all alone, Lugalbanda? What news?"

"I bring a message from the king," said the little prince. "Once, long ago, you summoned him to this place when it was just a marsh. You had him drain the land and build the city and rule the people with justice and peace. All this he did as you asked. So why have you abandoned him now in his struggle to conquer Aratta? Why have you left him there and come back to Uruk? What has he done?

"King Enmerkar begs great Inana, that even if you have no further use for him you will at least bring him and all his troops safely home to Uruk. Then he will lay down his spear and you can break his shield and he will make an end to war."

The goddess replied with mysterious words in the way goddesses do. "By the banks of the river where the water meadows lie," she said, "there is a pool of sacred water where a little fish eats the honey weed, a larger fish eats acorns and the largest fish of all frolics and plays. Among the tamarisk trees that grow at the edge of the pool one stands alone. If King Enmerkar is to take the city, he must find the pool, cut down the lone tamarisk and make a bucket from its wood, catch the biggest fish and offer it to the gods. Then his troops may prevail and the battle-strength of Aratta will ebb away.

"But one thing he must understand: it is not for him to destroy Aratta! Only if he brings its worked metal, its fabled stone carvings and the

artists and craftsmen who made them to safety, only if he restores the place and settles it again, only then will King Enmerkar have victory and my blessing again."

And so it was.

Now the battlements of Aratta are made of lapis lazuli and its towering walls of shining brick from the iron-rich earth of the Zabu Mountains where the cypress trees grow.

Lugalbanda carried the goddess's message back over the mountains. His legs were strong and he never got tired, and he ran and he ran all the way back to where the fighting raged and the old king waited. And Enmerkar pondered the mysterious words of the goddess and understood a warning.

So he made his offerings to the gods and, when the fighting ebbed away and the gates of Aratta opened to the army of Uruk, King Enmerkar was wise. He did not destroy Aratta or reduce it to rubble. No, he restored the city from the damage of the war and settled it again and made sure its treasures and the craftsmen who made them were safe.

Then King Enmerkar returned to Uruk at the head of his army with Lugalbanda at his side and the seven brothers close behind. With them they brought stone and burnished silver and lapis lazuli and craftsmen from Aratta to teach the people of Uruk new skills. And when they reached the temple of Inana, the king laid down his spear at the feet of the goddess and she broke his shield to make an end to war.

The little prince got on with growing up in peace, and ran as far and as fast as he liked. And when he was grown, Lugalbanda, the favourite of Inana, became the next king of Uruk. But he kept his promise to the Anzu bird. All through the land of Uruk, woodcarvers and painters, stonemasons and metalworkers made beautiful statues of the Anzu bird, singers sang songs about him and story-tellers told this story again and again so that no one would forget. ❖

NOTES · ON · THE · STORY

Lugalbanda was the third king of the first dynasty of Uruk. He succeeded Enmerkar, who may have been his father, and was in turn succeeded by Gilgamesh, who is thought to have been his son.

More than five thousand years ago, the great Sumerian city-state of Uruk which they ruled was not only one of the earliest cities in the world, but also the largest of Sumer's temple communities. Around 3000 BCE it comprised more than 100,000 inhabitants, 400 hectares of city and a 9 kilometre surrounding wall. This was a phenomenal achievement and one not matched anywhere in the world for hundreds, if not thousands, of years. As for Aratta, though its location is unknown, the Zabu and Lullubu mountains are thought to be part of what are now the Zagros Mountains in Iran.

What's extraordinary is that, as recently as 150 years ago, nobody had any idea that the Sumerians even existed. Who were they? It's hard to be sure. Neither the people nor the language seem to be connected with any others recorded. Their civilization emerged in the flat plains of what is now southern Iraq more than 6,000 years ago and flourished for nearly 2,000 years before it was absorbed into the Babylonian and other cultures which followed. Then it disappeared.

But what a civilization it was. Not only did the Sumerians have cities, they had law, literature, mathematics, science. From them we get our divisions of time – 60 seconds to the minute, 60 minutes to the hour, 24 hours to the day, 12 months to the year. They were the first to harness animals to the plough. They developed wheeled vehicles and boats with sails. And what really made the difference was their invention of writing – writing on clay. Unlike paper, papyrus or cloth, clay lasts. When cities burn, clay lasts even better. Almost everything the Sumerians wrote down survived, even though it was buried for up to 4,000 years.

It is in Uruk that the world's first writing is found, dating from about 3100 BCE; and later, around 2600 BCE, not just lists and accounts, but the first human literature: hymns and stories and poems like this one, vivid with imagery. Although spoken Sumerian died out around 1700 BCE, for centuries afterwards written Sumerian continued to be used as the language of scholarship (much as Latin was used in the Middle Ages) by the people who came after, and its cuneiform writing was adopted by other languages. But when cuneiform too died out, around 100 CE, all connection was lost.

It was only in the mid nineteenth century that the rediscovery began. In 1849 and 1852 an Englishman called W. K. Loftus, excavating at Warka in Iraq, discovered the remains of Uruk. But it wasn't until the 1920s and 30s that a German expedition revealed the extent of what was really there, and the tablets which turned out to include the first part of this story. In 1888 an expedition from the University of Pennsylvania led by John Punnet Peters dug up a huge library at Nippur containing thirty to forty thousand clay tablets. These, and huge numbers of other broken clay tablets, were sent back from excavations in the near East to museums in London, Paris, Berlin, Istanbul, Philadelphia, Chicago and elsewhere. And there they sat: indecipherable.

Unlike monumental slabs or carved stone inscriptions, clay tablets don't look like much. Crumbling biscuits of clay, almost indistinguishable from the brick rubble where they are found, they vary in size from something that would fit in the palm of your hand to pieces the size of a large page. It took a further hundred years for scholars in Germany, Turkey, France, Britain and the United States to decipher the cuneiform script and then the Sumerian language and begin the painstaking work of translation. It was only in the 1970s that the first translations of the Lugalbanda poems were assembled. And this is just the beginning. Today there are still many thousands of untranslated tablets in museums around the world and who knows how many more still buried in the sands of Iraq.

I came to these stories through the work of my friend, the oral story-teller Fran Hazelton, who specializes in telling ancient Mesopotamian stories in English to adult audiences. These powerful epics and fragments about war and gods and love

and death are no children's stories, nor do they conform to modern narrative requirements. Without authors, or dates, we know remarkably little about them. And yet they speak. And with an immediacy which is breathtaking.

So when, just before the 2003 invasion of Iraq, I came across the story of Lugalbanda, it hit me like a thump in the chest. This was much too important to be left to the world of adults. And so the project began.

Lugalbanda's story is recorded in two separate poems, known as "Lugalbanda in the Mountain Cave" and "Lugalbanda". The first, a single copy of 499 lines, was found in the excavation of the Temple of Eanna at Uruk. Dating from 2400 BCE, three hundred years before the earliest text of The Epic of Gilgamesh, it can well lay claim to be the oldest written story in the world. The second survives in twenty-two later versions from Nippur, Kish and Nineveh as well as Uruk, dating from between 2150 BCE and 1650 BCE, the main period of Sumerian written literature.